THE BRIDE TAKES A STAND

MAIL ORDER BRIDES OF WYOMING

SUSANNAH CALLOWAY

Tica House
Publishing

Sweet Romance that Delights and Enchants!

PERSONAL WORD FROM THE AUTHOR

Dearest Readers,

Thank you so much for choosing one of my books. I am proud to be a part of the team of writers at Tica House Publishing who work joyfully to bring you stories of hope, faith, courage, and love. Your kind words and loving readership are deeply appreciated.

I would like to personally invite you to sign up for updates and to become part of our **Exclusive Reader Club**—it's completely Free to join! We'd love to welcome you!

Much love,

Susannah Calloway

VISIT HERE to Join our Reader's Club and to Receive Tica House Updates!

https://wesrom.subscribemenow.com/

CONTENTS

CHAPTER 1

On the day when everything changed, Isabelle Altman had stars in her eyes.

It was the end of the summer season in Boston, and the city in which she had been raised had never appeared more beautiful. The skies were a clear blue, arching over head as though gravity were little more than a quaint idea. Down the street from the little flat she shared with her aunt, the trees of the park were just beginning to be tinged with color. The world felt as though it stood on the brink of something wonderful, and she was heartily glad to be alive.

Twenty years old, with a pretty face, a new dress, a supper party to go to, and only a jovial aunt to rein her in, Isabelle felt keenly that the world was her oyster.

But that was before she arrived at the Beckwood mansion, and everything turned topsy-turvy.

It was in Adam Beckwood's demeanor that she first noticed the difference. Adam was only a few years older than she was herself, the pride of the Beckwood family. His younger sister, Lydia, had gone to school with Isabelle. With more cunning than Isabelle would have credited her with, Aunt Imogen had insisted that Isabelle cultivate the friendship, and though Isabelle was not particularly close with Lydia, she did enjoy at least the edges of the Beckwood social circle.

The Altmans had never been well-to-do, though neither were they ever beholden to their debtors. Isabelle's father had passed when she was young, leaving her to the care and keeping of his younger sister, with the help of a modest monthly income. No, Isabelle had never felt the need to seek a fortune in marriage, but the possibility of marrying into one wasn't exactly a negative thing, either…

Adam had always seemed to be partial to her, though he didn't pay her much more attention than he did any of the other girls his younger sister spent time with. But he'd always had a smile for her.

Until tonight.

Stepping inside the spacious foyer of the Beckwood home, she spotted Adam near the entryway into the dining room. She smiled brightly and lifted a hand to wave even as she removed her cloak, but the expected smile in response did not appear. Instead, he merely lifted one elegant black brow, as though acknowledging a distant acquaintance with the bare minimum of politeness needed in order to avoid an overt snub and turned back to the young woman who stood near him. There was an undeniable strain to the set of his mouth, indicating displeasure.

A mass of dark, curly hair pinned up but with locks spilling over in the latest fashion, a dove gray dress of watered silk – she recognized the form of May Townsend, another old classmate, and a much closer friend than Lydia Beckwood. The sight was a relief to her. May would make her feel better, no matter what silliness Adam indulged himself in. Despite the quale of her heart at Adam's strange behavior, Isabelle started forward to greet her friend. But before she could reach them, Adam took May's arm and led her away, over the threshold into the dining room.

Halfway across the foyer, Isabelle hesitated. Surely something must be wrong – but she couldn't think what. She turned hastily to the full-length mirror that decorated the far wall and surveyed herself anxiously. The blue dress her aunt had insisted on paying for this past season was slightly out of fashion, but certainly not enough for Adam to turn up his nose at, and she wasn't entirely sure that men noticed that sort of thing, anyhow. Her blonde hair was pinned up, not a strand out of place; it was straight as a stick and very long, so she hadn't bothered to try the same sort of hairstyle that May was sporting this evening. Her cheeks were healthily pink after the walk from her aunt's home to the Backwoods, but overall, everything seemed to be just as she would have expected.

Frowning at herself and not nearly as reassured as she had hoped, she turned away from the direction of the dining hall and went instead to the right, towards the receiving room. She was far from the first one there. Dozens of other partygoers had already arrived, many of them clustered in little knots sprinkled throughout the receiving room and the ballroom beyond. She spotted Mrs. Beckwood herself holding court in the far corner, and when their eyes met, she gave the woman a deep nod and smile of appreciation and greeting. Her heart did a little somersault to see that she received in return only a cold nod.

But then, Mrs. Beckwood had always secretly believed that Isabelle was no better than she should be, coming from a family that was rather less wealthy than Mrs. Beckwood's. Perhaps it wasn't such a secret; Isabelle had heard as much both from May and from Lydia Beckwood herself, over the years.

Despite that, Mrs. Beckwood had always been the height of politeness, and this frigid acknowledgement only added to the confusion in Isabelle's mind. She set to searching out someone who might set her mind at ease, but friend after friend gave her little more than a distant greeting, and more than a few of them accompanied this with stares of outright curiosity.

By the time twenty minutes had gone by, Isabelle's nerves had been sorely tried. She made her way from the rarified air of the receiving room into the ballroom, which was still relatively uncrowded as the music had not yet started. The quartet was warming up in the corner, and she searched through the sparse listeners for a familiar face – or better yet, a friendly one.

To her surprise, it was Lydia Beckwood who appeared as though from nowhere, seized her arm, and dragged her off behind a potted plant in one of the cunningly concealed alcoves with which the ballroom was dotted.

"You did come," she said. "I half expected that you wouldn't, and, of course, Mother thought there wasn't a chance that you would."

Isabelle blinked at her.

"But – you sent me an invitation, didn't you?"

"Of course – a month ago, when Mother first planned the supper."

Isabelle gave a slight laugh of relief. "Oh, good. I'm glad to hear it. I was beginning to think I had imagined it. Lydia, what's wrong with everyone? Why am I being stared at by some and ignored by others? Why, even your brother didn't deign to speak to me – has something happened that I'm unaware of?"

Lydia stared at her with wide eyes, chewing on her fingernail for a moment as though unsure of what to say – or of how to say it.

"I thought perhaps someone would have told you," she said at last.

"Told me about what?"

"About – the rumor."

Isabelle stared back, her heart beginning to sink.

"What rumor?"

Lydia began to pace, wringing her hands.

"About a week ago," she said, "someone – a friend – came to Mother and told her that she was…" She swallowed hard. "Woefully mistaken in her estimation of you."

"What do you mean?" Isabelle shook her head. "I'm afraid I don't believe that your mother has much of an estimation of me to begin with, but I'm not sure…"

"Oh, Mother doesn't really like anyone," Lydia said swiftly. "That's nothing new. But she agreed to your company because she knew that you are one of my oldest friends – and as long as Adam didn't set his sights on marrying you, she didn't mind that you were around."

"That's…very kind of her," murmured Isabelle, wondering

whether she ought to be more upset about this condescension or about the unknown rumor.

"It was because you were known to be, if not rich, then at least solvent that she was amenable to your being a part of our social circle. But this friend said that they had it on good authority that you were not solvent at all. They stated that your father was deeply in debt when he died, and that you live on your aunt's charity alone – and that your aunt is soon to run out of money."

Isabelle's eyebrows lifted nearly to her hairline.

"What? Why on earth would anyone say such a thing?"

"And furthermore," Lydia went on, still wringing her hands, "that you were out to convince Adam to marry you – however you might have to force the issue." Her blue eyes pleaded with Isabelle, and Isabelle understood the meaning behind the words. There were ways to entrap a man into marriage – though the suggestion would never have crossed her mind, and it was horrifying to think that anyone would make such an accusation, especially in the presence of Mrs. Beckwood – and perhaps even Adam himself.

She opened her mouth – then realized that the only thing she wanted to do was scream. That certainly would bring more attention to her – attention that she did not want. She closed her mouth again hastily and tried to regain her composure.

"It isn't true," she said, when she could manage to speak calmly, despite the wild beating of her heart and the shameful blush heating her cheeks. "Not a bit of it."

Lydia sighed and stepped forward, reaching out to grasp her hands.

"I thought not," she said. "And I said so – but Mother said that I couldn't prove it, because you and I were only in school together for the last two years before I went to finishing school. I said we ought to ask your aunt, but Mother said she wouldn't stoop so low as to investigate such a thing. I said we ought to ask you, at the very least, but – but Mother seemed to believe it without question, and…" Agitated, she began to wring Isabelle's hands instead of her own. "And no one would listen to me."

Isabelle took a deep breath, trying to steady her own nerves.

"Lydia," she started, "I won't pretend that I don't know that your brother would be an advantageous match for anyone – especially for a girl who lives in poverty. But I've never wanted for anything, though I've never been as wealthy as your family. I like Adam because he is Adam, and because we have spent time together. But if he doesn't care for me, I certainly won't lose any sleep over it." She shook her head, carefully loosening Lydia's clasp on her hands to put a hand to her forehead, trying to think. "I doubt that your mother would take my word for it – and perhaps not even the word of my aunt. I admit I'm not inclined to request Aunt Imogen to come and defend her financial situation in front of any accuser; it seems awfully undignified, and a poor return for her kindness to me ever since Father died."

"Yes, I know," Lydia whispered, her mouth twisting. "I'm sorry, Isabelle. I don't know of a way out of this. Mother wanted to disinvite you from the party – the only reason she didn't was because Adam insisted that you wouldn't have the courage to show up after all, once you realized that your secret was found out."

Isabelle shook her head firmly.

"Well, that's just silly," she said. "There was no secret to be discovered. I'm no more and no less than what I appear to be, Lydia – and I've only ever been honest with you and your family." She thought hard, her mind racing. "I know what to do. May Townsend is here – you know she's known me ever since we were little girls, for her mother was a maid in my aunt's house when we were young. Your mother can ask her. She'll tell the truth – and she knows it, too, for there were no secrets in my aunt's house."

Lydia's face went white, and she shook her head.

"I'm afraid we can't do that, Isabelle."

"Why ever not?"

"Because," Lydia whispered in anguished tones, "it was May herself who told Mother."

CHAPTER 2

"And now, here you are, Isabelle Altman," Isabelle whispered to herself, staring out the window, "starting off on a grand new adventure…" The corners of her mouth turned down, wryly. "And leaving your old life behind…for better or for worse…"

For richer, for poorer. In sickness, in health.

The litany of wedding vows echoed through her mind, and she slumped back in her seat, resting her forehead on the cool glass of the window with a sigh. Perhaps she should have let Aunt Imogen come with her on the journey to Wyoming, after all. The older woman loved the idea of traveling further than she ever had before – and doubtless she would never get the chance again. But train tickets for a journey of this magnitude were expensive, and Isabelle knew that Aunt Imogen's expressed desire to travel along with her was more for Isabelle's benefit, not Imogen's own. Aunt Imogen had done so much for her already – she couldn't allow her to do something so challenging, so difficult, so expensive.

The thought of the question of expense made her wince, even now.

A month had passed since that disastrous evening when she had first started to realize that her life was changed forever. Oh, she had done her best to put the rumors to bed; Lydia had helped, in her own way. But even when Mrs. Beckwood had unbent so far as to greet her at the next gathering, there had still been a cold suspicion in her gaze. And Adam was downright awkward, in a way that let Isabelle know he had his own suspicions still and had not yet made up his mind. May Townsend was ever on his arm these days; no doubt she was helping to fuel his confusion.

It was Aunt Imogen who had brought clarity to the situation – for Isabelle, at least, if not for anyone else.

"Of course, that little minx had to spread a rumor about you, my dear," she had said, when Isabelle came home that first awful evening to cry into the sofa pillows. "She's been after Adam Beckwood herself, and everyone knows that he wouldn't look at anyone but you. And what lie did she tell? Only a lie that reflects the truth of her own situation. Her mother was a maid in my household, you know – not that

14

there's anything wrong with good, honest work, but it certainly isn't the behavior of a wealthy woman. And I hear her father was a bit of a gambling man, in his day. No doubt little Miss May has her own debts to pay off, and the only way she can secure her own future is to destroy yours. Oh, now, my dear – don't cry, don't cry. She's not worth the tears. None of them are."

Aunt Imogen's voice had been strong and bitter, like tea left to steep too long. Isabelle couldn't help but wonder whether her aunt, who had started off an old maid and had finally reached an age that justified the term, had her own similar past experiences that colored her words.

But that was a thought that came later, when she had recovered somewhat. That first evening, she had been too distraught to think of anything but her own misery.

"But how will I face them again?" she moaned into the pillow. "Even if I could tell them the truth outright – and I can't do anything so low-class as to defend myself, or my father, against such accusations. Why, the Beckwoods never speak of money. Rich people never do."

"They needn't," said her aunt candidly. "Only poor people are on speaking terms with money, strangely enough. But listen, my dear, you needn't worry. The rumors will pass off soon enough…"

In her heart, Isabelle knew that her aunt was right. She could weather the storm, as she had weathered others – the death of her mother when she was little more than an infant, the death of her father five years after that, and a dozen other smaller tragedies that shape the lives of young women, outside of their control. But this one – this was different. She knew that she was fortunately placed to be inside the Beckwoods' social circle at all. And she knew, too, that no one within that same circle would ever view her in quite the same way. She couldn't bear it – and it was her aunt, once more, who came to the rescue with a new suggestion.

"Marriage," she had said promptly. "If you think that Adam Beckwood still believes you're setting your cap for him, and it embarrasses you – why, marrying someone else is the best response, isn't it?" She had chuckled dryly. "Think how much egg that young man will have on his face, to hear that you've turned his apologies down flat to marry someone else. And what's more, he'll end up having to marry May Townsend – and won't he be sorry then."

It was Aunt Imogen, too, who had crafted the plan that led her to this very train car. The matrimonial agency on Wheaton Street had played an instrumental role – and with Aunt Imogen's eager coaching, not more than two weeks had passed between Isabelle's public embarrassment and the announcement that she was engaged to a well-to-do rancher in Wyoming.

Aaron Granger.

The thought of him made her sigh again, and she closed her eyes to imagine him all the better. The matrimonial agency had furnished her with only a few sparse details, enough that she supposed she would recognize him when she saw him, at the end of this long journey. He was tall, a few inches over six feet, and broad-shouldered. His hair was fair, his eyes blue. He would be wearing a brown wool coat and a black hat when he came to greet her.

She didn't suppose that there would be too many other men waiting on the train platform in Millville, Wyoming who would meet the same description.

In a town as small as Millville sounded to be, she didn't suppose there would be too many other folks waiting on the platform at all.

The idea of getting used to a town only a smidgen of the size of the city she had always lived in was growing less and less intimidating, the more she thought of it. There would be fewer people to befriend, a smaller social circle, that much was true.

But there would also be fewer people to betray her, too. Fewer people to whisper behind her back. She flinched at the thought. Though she knew she should simply put May Townsend out of her mind entirely, it still hurt to think of how her childhood friend had destroyed her reputation – and purely out of greediness for her own ends, as far as anyone could tell.

She would never make the same mistake of trusting someone so implicitly, she promised herself.

The thought of what she had left behind pursued her over the next few weeks, as the train made its slow and laborious journey west. Along with the memories, which ran rampant through her mind and invaded her dreams, she poured her vibrant imagination into thinking of what her new life would be like. She wrote letter after letter to her aunt, with no real intention of posting any of them – it helped her to solidify her dream for the future, to write down the details.

As the landscape rolled by and the winter storms came and went, she fell to a rhythm of watching from the window, finding inspiration in some fleeting vision of the beauty of nature, and scribbling hastily on the page in front of her. Beneath her eager fingertips, the world she looked forward to took shape: a world in which she was loved and safe and cared for, and where adventure was at hand around every corner. A world in which she was wife and someday mother, a beloved part of the town that would become her own. She could see this almost as clearly as she could imagine what Aaron Granger must look like – a quaint little hometown, Millville, with everyone nodding and smiling as they passed by. Peace and harmony and happiness.

So different from what she had left behind, where one rumor could cause such discord.

As her destination drew closer, her daydreams more often were pleasant imaginings of the future ahead, and less often of the painful memories of the past. It was just as Aunt Imogen had promised her – striking out for something new and better would replace the old, if she would only let it.

The journey was far from easy. On the highest hills, it was as though autumn had already given way to winter; snow lashed the windows, driven by howling winds, and the train slowed to a crawl, and then a stop. They spent two cold days waiting for the tracks to clear enough to carry on; Isabelle huddled underneath her blanket in her little bunk, grateful for the furs that her aunt had insisted she take with her, though they were family heirlooms and had belonged to Imogen's great-grandmother.

Though the family had never been wealthy – and that was the last thing she cared about now, embittered by May's claims - she couldn't help but be glad to the heart that Imogen had had enough money to pay for space in a sleeper car for her only niece. Isabelle couldn't imagine the misery of waiting out the storm crouched in one of the hard chairs in the passenger cars, as those who were less well-funded were forced to do. Yes, money had its place, to be certain – but it certainly wasn't the be-all and end-all, as May Townsend seemed to believe.

By the time the snow allowed them to continue onwards and they reached the plains once more, Isabelle realized that her long journey had gained an additional week. It wasn't until this fact washed over her that she also realized just how eager she was to reach her destination – and start her life anew.

As the train sped ever onwards over the plains, with mountains behind and more mountains ahead, she closed her eyes and remembered to breathe a prayer of thanks for everything that had brought her to this moment.

And another prayer for Aunt Imogen – and her brilliant ideas.

CHAPTER 3

Isabelle arrived in the friendly, peaceful little town of Millville, Wyoming, in the midafternoon of a Tuesday in late November.

Stepping off the train, she set her bag down for a moment and took in a deep breath. Millville was situated on the plains in a little cup between mountain ranges, as though held in the palm of a gigantic hand. It was high enough in elevation that there was a tinge of frost in the air, though the sun was shining brilliantly overhead. Under the incandescent light, the town looked picturesque, the very image of what she had been imagining.

Except for one thing – the faces of the few folks who were passing by were not as friendly as she would have expected. Or as she would have hoped.

In fact, she got nothing but wary glances everywhere she looked.

Well, she told herself, bending to pick up her bag once more, perhaps that was only to be expected, really. A town this size couldn't see many visitors – though she did feel rather self-conscious, almost the way she had felt on that disastrous evening at the Beckwoods'. She ran a hand over her hair, to make sure that it hadn't come loose and wild, but everything felt in place beneath her bonnet. The same was true of her dress, when she smoothed a hand quickly down her skirts. Everything seemed to be where it ought.

Except, of course, for Aaron Granger.

A tall man with broad shoulders, wearing a brown coat and a black hat, was nowhere to be seen.

In fact, there were no men at all to be seen there on the platform, and precious few visible walking down the street in the distance.

Perhaps that was only to be expected, too, she reminded herself. After all, the train was a week later than it was supposed to be – though it certainly seemed as though the town might have been warned that it was coming through late. Suppose someone wanted to continue west? How would they know when to buy a ticket or be ready to travel?

Then again, it didn't appear that anyone was anxious to leave

Millville. She was the only one who disembarked at the station. And no one else took her place.

Sighing, she put all of this aside as a conundrum that she would puzzle over later, when she had the leisure time. Now, the question was how to locate the man who was to be her husband.

She made her way to the street nearest to the platform, and turned to the left, searching the painted signs above each doorway for something that looked likely to be able to furnish her with the information she needed. The mercantile was the first building she passed – but the windows were dark, and it appeared that it had closed for the day, though it was still relatively early. Stranger still, one of the plate glass windows was clearly broken, half of it boarded up with rough-cut planks.

She hesitated there for a moment, peering inside, and her heart jumped to see someone peering back at her. He stood behind the counter – but he made no move to come to the door, and after a moment she went on, feeling more unnerved by the moment.

The next place was a dress maker's shop – and she didn't think it very likely that anyone within would know the whereabouts of a bachelor rancher.

The next building bore a sign that declared it the residence and office of Doctor Andrew Bittern. With a sense of relief, she opened the door and went in. Here, at least, she should be greeted with common courtesy.

The doctor himself proved to be an elderly fellow with a gigantic white mustache; she knew this at once, as he was in the waiting room, seated beside a young male patient and winding a bandage around his temple. He glanced up and gave Isabelle a concerned frown before nodding to a chair, then returned to his business. She took a seat, her bag at her feet, and waited with her hands in her lap while the doctor completed the bandage and stood up, helping the young man to his feet in turn.

"Now, go on home and try not to get trampled again, Jerry," he said. "The next time they won't go so easy on you."

Jerry cast a swift glance at Isabelle, a mixture of curiosity and suspicion, and went on his way, already picking at the bandage.

"And don't pick at it."

The last they heard of Jerry was a fierce mutter that Isabelle couldn't quite make out. The doctor heaved a sigh and turned to her at last, shoving his hands in the front pockets of his rather dingy white coat.

"And what can I do for you, miss? We don't see many strangers around here. It's a shame that your visit must start out in my office. Not that I'm not glad to see a pretty face," he added, chuckling dustily. "Few enough of those around, and at my age, a fellow appreciates 'em more than ever."

"That's very kind of you," Isabelle said, blushing a little. She could tell that the old man meant it teasingly, though he seemed to be in earnest at the same time. Whatever the truth of the matter, he was harmless. "But I'd be more grateful for your kindness in another way."

"Oh? What's that, m'dear?"

"I'm looking for Mr. Granger, Mr. Aaron Granger. He has a ranch around Millville."

The doctor sat back in his chair, both bushy eyebrows climbing his forehead in surprise.

"Aaron, eh?" he said. "Well, miss, if you'd been here a few days ago you would have seen him sittin' in that chair right next to you – along with all those other rascals who keep gettin' 'emselves into trouble." He scoffed. "But now, I reckon he hasn't gotten out of bed since I turned him loose, let alone left the house. So, you'd do best to start your search there."

She gaped at him.

"You don't mean he's – bed-ridden?"

"If he isn't, he's an even greater fool than I give him credit for," said Doctor Bittern.

"But – what's wrong with him?"

"Oh, nothin' that time won't cure, I expect. Well, time or a more accurately fired arrow." He scoffed again, huffing into his mustache. "He ought to know to leave well enough alone, but when Henry Parish calls for help…"

She held up a hand, feeling rather overwhelmed.

"Who is Henry Parish?"

The doctor leaned back in his chair, crossing one leg over the other. He drew a pipe from his pocket, filled and tamped it slowly, then lit it with a match struck against a thumbnail. With slow deliberation, he took a few puffs, eyeing her all the while.

"You really ain't from around here, are you, miss?"

She pressed her lips together, hoping her frustration didn't show too baldly.

"That's right, I'm not."

"Otherwise, I reckon you'd know Henry Parish, seein' as he's only the richest rancher in the whole of the county. Maybe all of Wyoming itself. And always on the verge of gettin' richer, if he has his way about it. Say, who are you, anyhow, miss? And what are you doin' looking for a man like Aaron Granger?"

She took a deep breath.

"My name is Isabelle Altman, from Boston, Massachusetts," she said. "I've come here in response to an arrangement by a matrimonial agency – an arrangement between Mr. Granger and me. I only know what the matrimonial agency has told me about him – that he's a rancher here in Millville. I don't know where he lives, or I wouldn't have bothered you."

The doctor waved a hand.

"Oh, it ain't no bother, miss – Miss Altman, was it?"

She nodded.

"Well. I see. Miss Altman…" He hesitated, his gray gimlet eyes still fixed on hers, and she sensed that though his appearance was harmless, even rather humorous, he was far more intelligent than he let on. He seemed on the verge of telling her something vastly important, and she leaned forward to hear it from him – but at the last moment, he seemed to change his mind and switched tracks abruptly. "Why don't I just tell you where Aaron's little homestead is and send you on your way. It'll be dark soon, Miss Altman, and you'll have to walk quickly if you want to get there before twilight sets in."

She sat back, nodding gratefully, despite her disappointment. She had so many unanswered questions – who exactly was Henry Parish, this "richest rancher in the county," and why had Doctor Bittern expected her to know him? What had he to do with Aaron Granger? And what had landed Aaron Granger in the doctor's office days before, to be followed by him being bedbound?

The doctor was bent over the little table in the corner, scribbling directions with a practiced hand. Isabelle stood and reached out to him.

"Doctor…"

"Hmm?"

"What's wrong with Mr. Granger?" she asked, eyes fixed steadily on his. "Why was he here in your office? What can I expect to find, when I go to him?"

The doctor eyed her for a moment and then chuckled again, handing her the folded piece of paper.

"Now, that would be tellin'," he said, laying a finger alongside his nose and winking at her. "Go on with you, Miss Altman. You'll make it in plenty of time, if you hurry."

What she really wanted to do was to sit him back down and press him to tell her what he knew – but she had a feeling that any such attempt would be completely fruitless. Doctor Bittern struck her as the stubborn type.

But then, she reminded herself, so was she.

Though crabbed and spiky, the doctor's handwriting was relatively easy to make out, his directions surprisingly simple to follow. She made her way back along the path she had taken, noting again that though there were quite a few passers-by, they almost all gave her looks of mingled curiosity and suspicion, as though reluctant to believe that she might have upfront and honest motivations for being in their little town.

She couldn't help but wonder at this. She had expected friendliness, and here no one seemed ready even to say a greeting to her. Even more than that, folks seemed inclined to scurry along the pathways, as though expecting some disaster to strike while they were out and about, without protection. She noted also that there were few women and children who were not accompanied by men.

What sort of place had she come to? It was clearly far from the peaceful region she had expected.

Mystified and more than a little unnerved, she followed Doctor Bittern's directions just outside of town, where one final turn onto a short dirt road led her to a small, well-kept farmhouse. All of Aaron Granger's acreage must have extended behind the house, she thought, doing a little bit of snooping as she made her way up the pathway. Around the corner of the house, she could make out a spread of grasses, a meadow carpeted in golden-headed grains, dotted by black and brown cows. A few spreading oaks offered shelter from the sun or rain, as needed; it was beautiful and strikingly peaceful, especially compared to the air of breathless anticipation that had permeated what she'd seen of Millville.

She held her own breath as she knocked on the door of the house.

There was a long silence, and then a wary voice called, "Come in."

Isabelle gripped the handle of her valise tightly in one hand and pushed the door ajar. She stepped just inside the house, her vision sweeping it side to side, taking in the details – clean and simple, hardly a knickknack on the shelf, with a kitchen visible to the left and the foyer more of a sitting room. At the far end of the room, she saw the tall, stooped figure of a man.

She could not take the time to notice much about him or his appearance – her eyes were drawn at once to the unwavering muzzle of the black gun in his hands.

Behind the gun, his eyes were a startling blue, his hair tousled and tow-colored. He wore neither a black hat nor a brown coat, but she knew he must be Aaron Granger.

She froze where she was, any speech dying in her throat. Aaron made a small sound – was it disappointment? - and lowered the gun at once.

"Sorry," he said, and to her utter surprise he grinned sheepishly at her. "I'm afraid everyone's been a little touchy around here lately."

Isabelle swallowed past the lump in her throat and tried to pretend that her heart wasn't beating a hundred times per second. She stepped fully into the house, leaving the door open, and turned to face him.

"You must be Aaron Granger."

"Must be," he said, rubbing his bristly chin. "Days like this, I wish I wasn't, though. Who might you be, miss?"

"Isabelle Altman," she said faintly. "The matrimonial agency sent me."

Aaron Granger's face froze before melting into an expression of chagrin. He ran a hand through his hair, standing it up on end, and whistled – then let out a few muttered curses that made her blink.

"Sorry," he said again, holding a out a hand to her. "I plumb forgot, Miss Altman, and that's the truth. When Parish came to ask me to join his posse, I forgot just about everything else, I guess." He shook his head. "Not that it's any excuse. I owe you a dozen apologies – maybe even more. I'm awful sorry, Miss Altman. Will you come in? Come in and sit down. I'll fetch you some tea – or would you rather something else?"

"Tea would be fine," she said, moving across the little sitting room to the settee under the window.

He grinned again, even more sheepishly.

"Fact is, I reckon I only have coffee and whiskey, now that I think of it."

"Coffee, then."

She watched him for a moment as he moved towards the little kitchen, and stood up to follow him, alarm jolting through her. It was clear that he was not well, favoring his left foot. His right arm seemed to be troubling him, too, and he used it only gingerly.

"Mr. Granger – let me help. What's wrong? Did something happen?"

He raised an eyebrow at her as she hustled up to his side, taking his elbow to support him. He leaned against the wall on the other side.

"Why would you think that?"

It was rueful and wry, but she answered it truthfully.

"The doctor told me that you'd been in his office."

"Doc Bittern? When did you see him to speak to?"

"He's the one who told me how to find you. I arrived on the train several hours ago and didn't know where to go."

"Ahh," he said, grimacing as he put a little weight on his injured foot. "Well, it's better than it was a few days ago, so I reckon Doc Bittern knows what he's doin' after all. I twisted it in the stirrup."

"Really?" She blinked at him in confusion. "I wouldn't have thought that sort of thing happened to an experienced rancher – please, Mr. Granger, sit down, and I'll fetch the coffee." She eyed him closely. "Unless you would rather whiskey."

He grinned and shook his head.

"I reckon that's a test," he said. "And I refuse to fall for it. I'm not much of a drinker – though it did help the pain, I'll grant you that. You're right, Miss Altman, it's a rare rancher who stumbles around his horse. Except for when he's bein' attacked by a bunch of wild Indians, and the horse takes fright and starts to run while he's tryin' to mount."

She turned to him swiftly, her eyes wide.

"Is that what happened?"

He took the mug she offered him, nodding his thanks.

"The Lord's own truth," he said. "We were out past Henry Parish's place, scoutin' out the land he plans to acquire. They came after us."

"Who did?"

He swallowed deep of the mug, with a nod of appreciation and respect for the brew. "The Lakota." His eyes darted swiftly to hers, speculatively. "I don't reckon you've had much experience with the tribe, bein' from back east."

She shook her head.

"No, not really. Not any of the Indians – much. There was a fellow who worked for the green grocer's down the street – I believe he was an Indian. He never spoke to me – I don't know that he knew English. But he always had the kindest smile, rare as it was."

Aaron Granger gave a noncommittal grunt. "Well, be that as it may – I don't reckon these fellas were smiling, kindly or otherwise. Three of our gang ended up with arrows stickin' out of 'em. If they'd had access to firearms, I doubt that any of us would have survived to tell the tale. They're fierce, the lot of 'em."

Isabelle frowned at him. "They attacked you without any reason? Why would they have done that?"

He shrugged, clearly unwilling to speculate, but Isabelle's mind was churning. The image of men – ordinary men, regardless of their tribe and heritage – attacking others simply to cause a fight did not sit well with her. The only fights she'd ever witnessed had been caused by something, whether it be as insignificant as too much drink.

"And did your group wound them in return?" she pressed, but Aaron's handsome face bore an expression of mild annoyance, liberally laced with pain.

"I reckon we've got more important things to settle," he said. "I'd take you back into town to the boarding house, but the doc says I ought to give my ankle another day at least." He shook his head, mouth turning down ruefully. "Interfering with everything – the ranch, my cattle, and now a pretty girl."

Though her heart thrilled a little at the flattery, which seemed honestly meant, she tried to keep calm in her tone.

"I suppose we ought to settle our arrangements, yes. When will we marry?"

He shook his head again, immediately.

"Not until Parish and the rest of us sort out the danger," he told her. She eyed him in dismay.

"Why, when will that be?"

"Couldn't tell you. Not long, I hope. Not the way Parish operates," he added grimly.

"But…"

"Nadine Cobert will put you up. Just tell her that I sent you, and we'll settle accounts later. I reckon just about everyone in town knows I wrote for a bride." He smiled at her, and there was a sudden softness in his eyes. "And here she is. You're mighty pretty, Miss Altman."

She couldn't help but blush, this time.

"I suppose you ought to call me Isabelle."

"Well, if you suppose it, I reckon I ought. You strike me as the type that's usually right about things." He pushed up from the table, leaning on it with his left hand, his right arm slightly bent to avoid any pressure. She couldn't help but wonder if the twisted ankle was really his only wound. But he didn't seem inclined to share much more with her, and as she made her way towards the door with him shuffling slowly after her, she also couldn't help the doubts that crowded through her mind. Aaron Granger was handsome and stalwart, and likely he was a hard worker, too – but he was undoubtedly keeping something from her, and she didn't much care for the way he spoke of others.

She wondered what Aunt Imogen would say when she found out about how things were progressing.

Good old Aunt Imogen – it's your fault I'm here, mind.

She turned on the veranda to face him once more.

"Shall I return tomorrow?" she asked.

He scratched the back of his neck thoughtfully and then nodded.

"I reckon so," he said. "I won't be leavin' the house much, except to get back to work with the cattle. You're welcome to come spend time with me, if you like."

She offered him a hopeful smile.

"I will," she said. "We can get to know each other."

He gave her a long, hard look.

"That's right," he said. "We'll get to know each other."

But as Isabelle made her way back towards the main part of town, her heart was sinking slowly and steadily in his chest.

She was certain there had been doubt in his eyes – mirroring the doubt that was growing in her heart.

"Good old Aunt Imogen," she whispered ruefully.

CHAPTER 4

Nadine Cobert was just as standoffish as the rest of the townsfolk Isabelle had encountered up until then – until she heard Aaron Granger's name.

"Oh. Aaron sent you, eh?"

Isabelle nodded.

"He did."

"Well, then." Nadine looked her up and down, still speculatively, but with a more generous judgement than the first moment they'd laid eyes on each other. "You must be the girl he wrote to the matrimonial agency for."

It seemed an awful casual way to dismiss a match made by matrimonial experts – one which was theoretically destined to end in true love – but after everything she'd been through, Isabelle was not inclined to split hairs.

"Yes, I am," she replied steadily.

This unflappability, along with Aaron's name, earned her a welcome into the boarding house. She was shown to a room under the eaves – "I'm a little full at the moment, or I'd give you one on the first floor," the older woman explained – and given time to unpack and make herself comfortable before Nadine set a late supper for her. By this time, it was quite late, the sun having long descended over the mountains that surrounded the little town, and as Nadine told her, everyone else had already eaten.

Isabelle suspected that it was again due to Aaron's name that she was afforded such a concession – and as she herself had not eaten since very early that morning, she was in no mind to look a gift horse in the mouth. The plate of warmed-over stew and cornbread, with a cup of fresh hot coffee, was devoured within moments, and she bid goodnight to Nadine Cobert and made her way back to her room. She had scarcely undressed and washed up before she fell asleep, half in and half out of the covers on the little cot.

The next morning, she rose late, feeling refreshed despite a rather restless night. Making her way down to the dining room, she found a plate of cooling porridge waiting for her – but the coffee was as hot as ever, and that, Isabelle decided, was the important thing. She was lingering over the second cup when a young man entered the dining room, looking flustered. He raised his eyebrows in surprise to see a stranger there, but only gave her a polite nod before pushing on to the kitchen. From the open door, voices floated out to Isabelle's ears.

"There you are, Mitch. I've been wondering whether you might show up one of these days."

"Now, don't nag, Nadine – some things are more important than carryin' wood and fetchin' water."

Nadine gave an unladylike snort. "Like runnin' around after the likes of Henry Parish, I suppose."

"I'm not runnin' around after anyone," said Mitch defiantly. "Mr. Parish needs all hands on deck – all the help he can get. It's the right thing to do, as a resident of Millville. If we don't stand up for ourselves, those menaces out there'll go on the warpath."

"If Henry Parish would just leave well enough alone, we wouldn't have to worry about defending ourselves," said Nadine sternly. "He's greedy, that's what. Not like honest small-time ranchers, like Aaron Granger."

Isabelle leaned forward to listen, her interest piqued by hearing Aaron's name. She heard water splashing in the basin. Evidently Mitch was finally starting about his business in the kitchen, fulfilling his duties, but he was far from done with speaking at the same time.

"Say what you want about Mr. Parish, but Aaron was out there with the rest of us, just last week."

"He's civic minded, I'll give him that. And Henry Parish is not the sort of man to take no for an answer. But Aaron's a local man – not like Parish. He never pushed to take land that didn't belong to him."

"It's free for the takin' to any man with the courage to do it," said Mitch, splashing indignantly.

"What belongs to someone else ain't free to anyone," Nadine retorted. "Now, Henry Parish may not understand that, but it don't make it any less true. I was born and raised here in Millville, Mitch Drummond, same as you, only well before you were a twinkle in your daddy's eye. And there's never been trouble with the Lakota in the way there has been since the likes of Henry Parish started to buy up land – and get too big for their boots. If you men would let things lie, then we'd go back to bein' the most peaceful little place in all of Wyoming."

The last thing Isabelle heard from Mitch Drummond was a mutter under his breath, too low to make out the details of the words. She heard the kitchen door slam and presumed that one or the other of them had left, putting the contentious interview to an end.

She sat back, her coffee growing cold in front of her, forgotten, as her mind raced. So that was it. Mr. Parish evidently was one of the biggest landholders in the area –

41

Doctor Bittern's comments made that clear. But he wanted more, as rich men so often did. She spared a fleeting, bitter thought for Adam Beckwood, before her innate sense of fairness prompted her to admit that it was not just the wealthy who craved more than they possessed. It was the poor, too – after all, witness May Townsend.

How grateful she was, suddenly, that she had been raised by folks who knew where true value really lay. She herself had never wanted anything much – other than to love and be loved by others. And that sort of thing could not be purchased, regardless of how much land and wealth one had at their fingertips.

Aaron Granger had been involved in this fight with the Lakota – but Nadine clearly didn't hold him responsible the way she did Henry Parish.

With every answer she discovered, there seemed to be a dozen new questions on the horizon. She hurriedly found her cloak and boots and left, headed for the ranch, hoping to get the answers from Aaron himself.

He greeted her at the door with a smile that she could warm her hands at.

"You are real, after all. I was beginnin' to wonder whether I'd made you up in some delirium."

She smiled back, rather helplessly.

"I'm as real as they come, as they say – I'm sorry I didn't come back earlier, but I'm afraid I rather overslept this morning."

He shook his head, holding his door wide for her to step past him and enter.

"I reckon you needed the sleep, after that journey you had. Come on into the kitchen. Would you like some coffee? I made it myself, this time."

She shook her head.

"No, thank you, I had two cups at Nadine's."

"All right, come keep me company while I finish mine, then."

She took a seat beside him at the little kitchen table, and they fell into conversation with only a little awkwardness. It wasn't long before she was drinking her third cup of coffee. Aaron asked her how she found the boarding house, whether Nadine had treated her well, and if she'd been given supper the night before, despite the late hour. She put his fears to rest and asked a few questions of her own.

"Your ankle seems to be better."

He nodded, lifting it to twist in the air.

"Won't be bunny-hoppin' anytime soon, I guess," he said ruefully. "But I'll get by enough to catch up on chores around the ranch."

"May I help you with your chores? I ought to learn what needs to be done, anyhow, if I'm going to make this my home too."

He treated her to another one of those long, speculative looks that left her feeling rather red in the face.

"All right," he said at last, giving her a smile. "I reckon you're right, at that."

It was later, as they worked together to feed the cattle, that she mustered the boldness to ask him the question she most wanted to know.

"Aaron, you told me that you were attacked near Henry Parish's new acreage."

"Uh-huh."

"Something Nadine said made me wonder – does Mr. Parish own that acreage outright? Free and clear? Or does it belong to someone else?" Her heart was hammering a little, but she went on. "Someone like the Lakota."

He stopped and stared at her. A range of emotions ran across his face – some of them she recognized, like chagrin and then irritation – others, she could not put a name to. At last, he turned back to the task, reaching for a hay bale and hefting it.

"Used to, I guess," he said. "But it belongs to Henry Parish, now."

44

"And who decides that?"

He dropped the bale in its place, and turned to her, arms folded.

"What sort of questions are these?"

She gulped.

"I only want to know," she said.

"Want to know what?"

"The sort of town I will be calling my home."

He made a dismissive gesture. "That's got nothin' to do with it," he said. "Parish isn't Millville, and Millville isn't Parish. He's not the only person in town, and you oughtn't to define it by him. He ain't even from around here. Born in Wyeth, if I recall."

"But if his actions influence the town," she said gently, "then surely, it's important that I know. Nadine said that things were always peaceful between the settlers and the Lakota, before Mr. Parish arrived."

Aaron scowled at the bale of hay at his feet.

"Relatively, I guess," he said. "We didn't have attacks, that's for sure. I wouldn't say that we were all brothers – the Lakota keep to themselves. Always have, except for occasionally, you can see one of 'em watching from the woods, or a passel of 'em passing by the town on horseback."

He shook his head and sighed. "Maybe Parish does lead the charge, and maybe it ain't for the best. But progress must be made, Isabelle."

"At the expense of others?" she probed.

He pressed his lips together, keeping silent for a long moment.

"It ain't my decision," he said. "The only reason Millville is here is because settlers struck out into Indian territory, fifty years ago – I'm not sorry about it, and I can't pretend otherwise."

"No, I suppose not. But that hardly seems the same thing as what Mr. Parish is doing. He's reaching out for more land for himself, isn't he? Not for the other settlers." The word *greedy* nearly escaped her lips; it had been Nadine's word, and Isabelle kept herself from speaking it. Though she had her opinions, and her suspicions, she knew that it wasn't right to assume the worst about anyone all the same. "And Wyoming is such a big, wide place – surely, there's room for all."

Aaron's mouth was pressed thinly; he wanted to argue with her, she suspected, but there was something stopping him.

And she could guess what it was.

"I think you agree with me, Aaron," she said softly.

He turned his gaze from hers, and they were quiet for several moments, while the world slowly turned around them.

Then he took a deep breath and looked at her again, seeming to steel himself.

"I reckon you're right," he said. "You do need to know the sort of town you'll call home – and the sort of man you'll call husband, too. I have my principles, Isabelle Altman, and I stand by 'em. One of 'em is to come to the aid of those that ask for my help. Henry Parish asked for a hand. I couldn't turn him down – even if all I have to show for it is a twisted ankle."

She nodded, unwilling to push him any further. He showed great self-restraint, his voice calm and collected despite his obvious agitation – and she was more certain than ever that she was right. Despite his defense of the settlers, Aaron felt in his heart that to take land away from the Lakota was wrong – that was why he had made no attempt to do so himself.

He was trying to do what was right, even though it was difficult, the edges far from clear cut. And she couldn't help but admire that.

It told her a great deal about the man she was going to call husband, indeed.

But there was another side to the story, she knew – the side of the Lakota. And the clearest answer could not be reached until all narratives had been heard. That was when the idea entered her mind – she dismissed it almost at once, but it stayed with her, even as she spent the rest of the afternoon with Aaron, learning the ropes on the ranch and sharing an early supper with him before she returned to the boarding house. It was on the short walk back to her own bedroom that she faced up to it at last – she could do nothing about the situation without knowing the story from both sides.

And to do so, she must seek out the Lakota.

CHAPTER 5

It was Mitch Drummond who set her on the path towards Mr. Henry Parish's land, freely giving her the directions as though it was only natural that a newcomer to Millville should want to see the biggest spread in the county. She made her way north along the main pathway, reveling in the beauty of the autumn morning, and wondering how anyone would ever want to return to the city, once they had seen the mountains of Wyoming.

She certainly was not eager to do so – though she did rather miss her aunt.

The tumultuous relationship between the settlers and the Lakota was far more important than the gossip-ridden social imbalance in Boston, anyhow. It wasn't about something silly and simple, like who was setting their cap for whom. Despite the danger of what she was about to do, it made her feel rather glad not to have to contend with such issues any longer.

The Parish spread was easy to find. A path turned left off the main roadway, leading through a tall archway with the name Parish painted across it; to the left and right, split rail fences stretched, enclosing the acreage that Henry Parish so boldly claimed as his own. Isabelle left the main path and followed the right fence north, through the tall weeds and grasses. She was glad that it was rather chilly outside, autumn turning into winter earlier here in Wyoming, at this higher elevation, than it did back home in Boston. At least she didn't have to worry about stepping on any snakes.

She followed the fence for nearly an hour before it veered away, cutting across the field. Ahead of her she could see a swath of grasses cut trim, just as they were inside the fence – the work of men with scythes, she thought. A pile of logs lay ready, waiting to be split and placed to extend the fence. This was the land that Henry Parish was trying to claim.

She was drawing closer to the Lakota.

She continued, her heart beginning to pound. The meadows gave way to a stand of firs, thick and dark; she made her way around them for as long as she could before finally cutting through the first line. A brook meandered through, with thick grasses on either side and algae and moss nearly filling it; somewhere to the left was the river it met up with, though it was too far for her to hear the rushing of the waters. She splashed through the brook and continued.

Suddenly, it seemed unnaturally silent. Even the birds in the trees had gone still. She went still herself, holding her breath, her gaze sweeping through the tree trunks surrounding her. The hair on the back of her neck began to prickle – someone was watching her, she knew it. Someone that she could not see.

After a long, breathless moment – in which she began seriously to doubt the wisdom of her plan – a young girl stepped out from behind a tree.

One moment she was not there, and the next, she was. It was as though she had stepped from the tree itself, or as though the shadow of the great trunk had taken the form of a lithe figure. No, not a girl – a young woman, Isabelle realized. Her eyes were wide and dark, her long black hair loose around her shoulders. She wore buckskin leggings, a loose shirt made of what looked like linen, with a leather thong tied around her waist. She was barefooted and moved as though the earth below her feet were as soft as carpet.

Isabelle's mouth was dry, and yet she managed, "Hello…"

The girl tilted her head curiously, taking a step towards her.

"Hello," she said.

Isabelle's shoulders sagged with relief.

"Do – do you speak English?"

The girl shrugged, an elegant gesture. Now that she was closer, Isabelle judged her to be somewhere near her own age, perhaps a few years younger.

Did she know English? Her greeting had been delivered in a sure and certain tone, but her response to Isabelle's question was noncommittal in the extreme. If she did, how? Questions teemed in Isabelle's mind, but she knew that it was not the time to give vent to all of them.

"My name is Isabelle Altman," she said, pressing a hand to her chest. "I have come to speak to your people – on behalf of the people of Millville."

The girl tilted her head to the other side and eyed her sidelong.

"But you are not from Millville."

Her voice was clear, the words deliberate and well-chosen. Her accent was different from anything Isabelle had ever heard, but she showed not a hint of hesitation as she spoke.

And there was no arguing with her evident knowledge.

Isabelle took a deep breath and nodded.

"You're right," she said. "I've only just come here."

"Where are you from?"

"Boston – a very long way."

"Boston," repeated the girl thoughtfully. "I have heard of it – in the newspaper. Many stories are written of Boston."

Isabelle was still gaping at this unexpected comment when the girl stepped forward again and held out a hand.

"If you are a friend," she said, "then you may come with me. And I think that you are a friend."

Tentatively, Isabelle took her hand.

"What's your name?"

The young woman's teeth flashed white in her tanned face.

"Zonta White Bird," she said. "Zonta – it means *trustworthy*. Do you trust me, Isabelle Altman?"

Isabelle nodded.

"Yes," she said. "I trust you."

"Then come with me."

Zonta White Bird led her through the woods in silence, only pointing out a tree root her and there so Isabelle could avoid tripping over it. It was just as Isabelle was beginning to wonder how far they were going when they stepped out into a clearing and she caught her breath.

It was a town. A town of leather tents and log houses, of cooking fires burning and smoke lying low in the air, a town surrounded by trees and the majestic mountains stretching overhead, but a town nonetheless – with as many similarities to Millville as there were differences. The river ran through the clearing, at the far end of the little settlement. Zonta gave her a smile and led her through the groupings of tents toward the center. At every tent, every log house, Isabelle caught the eye of another Indian, most women, all watchful and wary.

She couldn't blame them. She felt a bit watchful and wary herself.

It was very similar to how she had been greeted at Millville – but this felt a bit more excusable. After all, she stood out like a sore thumb in the natural beauty of this place.

At the center of the town, one long, low building was placed, with the doorway covered with a leather flap. It was so low that even Zonta, who was a good few inches shorter than Isabelle, had to bend to go through it. She lifted it and called something that Isabelle could not understand, something in her own language, then went through, gesturing for Isabelle to follow.

Inside, an old man waited, an expectant expression on his weathered face. He sat cross-legged before a low fire; it was banked, but some smoke drifted up and through the hole cut in the roof. Feeling rather dizzy, Isabelle was grateful to be invited to sit. Zonta spoke rapidly to the old man, who nodded, though his face spoke volumes of his suspicion.

Zonta turned to Isabelle.

"This is Little Bear," she said. "He is my grandfather. He is the chief. I told him who you are, and where you are from. He speaks English, too," she went on, rather proudly. "I have taught him."

Isabelle couldn't help but smile at her even as she turned to the elder.

"Good morning," she said, faltering a little. How did one address an Indian chief politely? But she hadn't long to worry about it, for the old man responded almost at once.

"Good morning," he returned, nodding. "Zonta tells me you are from the town."

"Yes."

"And yet," he said softly, "you do not attack."

Isabelle's heart plummeted in her chest. With that simple sentence, she felt that all her suspicions about men like Henry Parish had been confirmed.

Still, she couldn't simply let it lie without questioning the assertion.

"I have heard," she said, feeling rather timid, "that it's your people who have attacked."

Little Bear closed his eyes.

"Sly Otter and his friends," he said. "When the rancher men were drawing close, they set upon them. And afterwards –

Sly Otter believes that if we show our strength in the town, they will stop taking our land. But I do not believe that."

"No?"

"No." He shook his head. "Because they have seen our strength – my father's strength, fifty years ago. And it did not stop them from taking our land." He opened his eyes. "But I will not let them take our village. The man Henry Parish wants this place, too. For the trees, the river. He will cut down the trees. He will dam the river."

Isabelle's throat ached. It wasn't the smoke. She turned to Zonta.

"It isn't everyone," she said urgently. "I haven't been here long, but I've heard enough to know that it isn't everyone. The townsfolk don't want to live in fear of being attacked – and they are content with what they have, from what I've heard. It's men like Parish that are causing the trouble. Isn't there anything that can be done?"

Zonta looked at her grandfather, who closed his eyes once more.

The young woman shook her head.

"Nothing can be done," she said softly. "Until the voices of the town are louder than the voices of the men – until the voices of peace are louder than the voices of battle."

Little Bear opened his eyes once more and looked down to the fire. He stirred it up with a stick, and sparks flew.

"It was good, that you came here, Isabelle Altman," he said. "But it is not enough."

Isabelle nodded. She looked back to Zonta, who was watching her, dark eyes bright.

"I'll do what I can," she promised. "Now that I understand."

Little Bear nodded.

"Broken bones call for mending," he said. "Zonta White Bird will take you back to your settlement. You are welcome here, Isabelle Altman – if you bring only peace."

This time, as they walked together through the village, the men and women of the tribe stood outside their tents and huts. But their faces were still full of suspicion.

"What should I do?" Isabelle whispered to Zonta. "How can I convince them that I mean no harm?"

Isabelle shook her head.

"There is no convince," she said. "There is only kindness."

"What do you mean?"

"Plant kindness," the girl said, throwing an arm out with her hand open as though scattering seed. "And trust that it will grow."

Isabelle smiled.

"That sounds like something my Aunt Imogen would say."

"She is a wise woman, your Aunt Imogen."

"Oh, very wise indeed."

They left the village behind and struck out into the woods.

"What did your grandfather mean?" Isabelle went on. "About broken bones?"

"He is a healer," Zonta told her. "He sees all evil, bad in the world as a sickness that needs healing. The connection between the people of the town and the Lakota was once strong – broken, when the settlers came, but wrapped and mended and whole. But now it is broken again, by men like Henry Parish. He does not understand." She turned to Isabelle, and again those white teeth flashed in a smile. "But you understand."

Isabelle took a deep breath.

"Yes," she said. "I understand."

CHAPTER 6

Over the next few days, Isabelle's life began to fall into a pattern.

She spent as much time as she could out and about in the little town of Millville, doing her best to befriend the people around her. They remained suspicious and wary – knowing what she knew now, about the dangers that had come upon them through the poor decisions of a few misguided men, she could understand why. But gradually, with the help of Aaron's name and Nadine's rather begrudging backing, she began to make inroads.

Still, when she broached the subject of the Lakota and the possibility of mending bridges, she almost invariably received little more than a hurried denial and a quick exit from the conversation.

It irked her, stirring her irritation – but the more she thought about it, the more she understood, and her sympathy was stirred in turn. The people of Millville were frightened. Some of their menfolk had been injured – arrow wounds, as Aaron had said, and as Doctor Bittern attested to when Isabelle went to speak to him. And though more than a few could remember the careful peace that had existed between Millville and the Indian village, prior to the arrival of Henry Parish, the wealthy rancher apparently wielded enough power that folks were reluctant to speak out against him, or to condemn his plan of seizing more land.

Like Aaron Granger, the people had their principles – but that didn't always extend to standing up for them, evidently.

What hope was there for peace, without courage to pursue it?

When she confessed what she had done to Aaron Granger, the light in his eyes told her of his irritation, though he did not speak it outright.

"You could have been killed," he said flatly.

She shook her head, watching him.

"You don't believe that," she said softly. "You've been here your whole life – Nadine said that it's only recently that there's been any battles with the Lakota. You know that they've been peaceful until provoked."

He stood, beginning to pace through the little kitchen. Even now, his ankle still troubled him, giving him a slight limp as he went; but it was the continued favoring of his right arm that worried her.

"Peaceful until provoked isn't peaceful at all," he argued. "You can't dismiss the fact that they shot at us, that men were wounded."

"Henry Parish was leading you to their village," she said. "That's what he wants – the very land they live on, the land they farm, the land where they raise their families. He wants to chase them out entirely. They only wanted to defend it."

"With violence?"

"Do men know any other way?" she cried.

He narrowed his eyes at her.

"Some folks would say they ain't men."

She caught her breath at the enormity of this – the wrongness of such an assertion ran through her like vibrating steel.

"But – not you, Aaron. You wouldn't say such a horrible thing."

His eyes fell before her beseeching gaze, and he wiped his mouth with the back of his hand as though the words themselves were bitter.

"No," he said. "I wouldn't. They're as human as anyone. Aw, hell, Isabelle, I know that they have a right to their own place, to keep their land. I don't agree with Parish tryin' to take their village – if I'd known, I wouldn't have ridden with him last week." He collapsed into his chair again, looking pale and spent, as though simply pacing and arguing had cost him a great deal. "He didn't say as much."

"Would you have expected him to?" she said. "It's an evil, evil thought. Perhaps he hasn't even admitted it to himself."

Aaron shook his head.

"I don't reckon Henry Parish thinks anything he says or does could possibly be wrong, let alone evil," he said. "The man is as full of pride as the river is full of water in February. I don't care for him much, and that's the truth – don't reckon anyone does. But we respect him, all the same. And he's part of Millville, even if he wasn't born and raised here."

She bit her lip. "I can understand that," she said softly. "I can even be grateful for it, I suppose. After all, I'm not from here, either – but I feel that the townsfolk are beginning to accept me."

Aaron glanced up at her, his wide blue eyes unexpectedly warm.

"I reckon they are," he said. "And I reckon they like you a great deal better than Henry Parish. If what Nadine tells me is anything to go by."

She looked down, fighting a blush, but giving in to a smile.

"You said that we couldn't marry until the danger was past," she said. "Until everything with the Lakota was sorted. But unless we all choose peace, instead of war, the danger will always be here."

Still, Aaron shook his head stubbornly, despite the warmth in his voice, in his eyes. He leaned heavily onto the table, and gave a yelp, sitting up straight again. Isabelle was on her feet and bending over him before she even knew it, reaching for him.

"What is it? What's wrong?"

He shook his head, muttering curses under his breath through gritted teeth.

"This damn arm of mine..."

"What is it, Aaron? Let me see."

Under her gentle pressure, he peeled down the shoulder of his flannel shirt far enough to reveal his bare upper arm, wrapped in bandages – bloody bandages. Isabelle let out an exclamation.

"You didn't tell me about this."

"Didn't want to worry you," Aaron said, gritting his teeth again as she turned him towards her, none too gentle in her agitation. "You figured it was my ankle that kept me close to home all this while – well, Doc Bittern didn't see fit to tell you that I was one of the wounded in the attack, so I figured I might as well keep it to myself as long as I could keep the cat in the bag. Now that it's out…"

She was on her knees before him, peering up beseechingly into his face.

"This is an arrow wound?"

He nodded.

She took a deep breath and removed the bandage as quickly and neatly as she could.

"I believe it's infected," she said. "I can clean it and bandage it up again, but you ought to go back to Doctor Bittern."

He shook his head.

"Doc Bittern did everything he could. He ain't as knowledgeable as some – especially not when he's in his cups."

She clucked her tongue, rummaging through the kitchen cupboard for the items she needed to care for the wound.

"Hold still," she told him softly.

He did – though she knew it must be painful.

"Why didn't you tell me that they had shot you?" she asked.

Aaron shook his head, his eyes clouded with sorrow and guilt rather than pain.

"I guess I reckoned I deserved it," he said at last. "Even before you told me that Parish was headin' for their village – I knew it was wrong, takin' their land. It's a conflict in me, Isabelle, in my insides. To fight at my brother's side, makin' his cause my cause – or to stand against him, makin' my principles his. Tryin' to, anyhow." He shook his head again. "It's a conundrum for a man. But I reckon you'd know what to do, wouldn't you?"

Their eyes met, and her heart beat so quickly and loudly that it sounded like fluttering bird's wings in her ears. She drifted closer to him without realizing it – and caught herself from reaching for him at the last moment.

After all, they were still just getting to know each other. And they could not set the date of their wedding until all this was settled.

So her growing attraction for Aaron Granger must be put to the side, she told herself sternly. There were much more important issues at stake here.

Much more important issues than her desire, every day stronger, to take him into her arms.

She drew a deep, rather ragged breath.

"Yes," she said. "I believe I know exactly what I would do."

Aaron's eyes fled from hers.

"I reckon that's what makes women stronger than men," he said. "The courage of your convictions."

CHAPTER 7

Two weeks went by, and nothing seemed to change.

Isabelle divided her days between time spent with others in the town and time spent at the little ranch with Aaron Granger. She felt that she was gradually coming to know the true makeup of Millville – there was a hardiness about the people who lived there, and a sense of community that she liked. Though everyone was clearly respectful of men like Henry Parish, who wielded more wealth and power than Isabelle felt was strictly good for them, it was just as clear that they reserved judgement on their morals.

A few, like Mitch Drummond, were all for Parish and the handful of other rich merchants and businessmen who made up his chief advocates; the unquestioning support of young men like Mitch Drummond was just as much a proof of their youth and idealism, Isabelle thought, as an indication of any innate greed. Powerful men tended to turn the heads of impressionable youngsters. It happened in Boston, and it happened here in Millville, too.

Once, after church on Sunday, she caught a glimpse of the man she knew must be Henry Parish, followed by a small group of sycophants and yes men, laughing raucously at some comment that had been made as he led the way into the saloon. She made sure to go the other direction. If she met Henry Parish, she could not guarantee her own good behavior.

She did not venture back to the Indian village – it felt almost shameful to return without any good news to bear. But she did go for a long walk in the woods and was not in the least bit surprised to be joined halfway through by Zonta White Bird, who gave her her usual gleaming smile and walked alongside in companionable silence.

Her yearning for Aaron grew by the day, and she had to admit to herself that though she wanted to make peace between Millville and the Lakota because it was the right thing to do, there was more than a little bit of selfishness to this urge, as well. She was falling in love with Aaron Granger, and he would not marry her until things were settled.

And so – she must do her best to ensure that things got settled, and quickly.

It was after the first real snowfall of winter that tragedy struck in the town. Isabelle knew little of it, at first; in the back of her mind, she realized that Mitch Drummond had not appeared at the boarding house for his kitchen boy duties in a day or two, but it wasn't until Aaron and Doctor Bittern appeared early one morning in search of her that she realized that there was more to his disappearance than the simple unreliability of the young.

One look at Aaron's face told her that something was badly amiss.

"What is it?" she asked, standing up from the table, her breakfast forgotten. "What's wrong?

Aaron stepped forward, glancing swiftly at the doctor, who nodded at him to carry on. The older man stood behind him, arms folded, and brow furrowed, as Aaron explained.

"Scarlet fever," he said. "At least, that's what the doc here reckons it is."

"It's unlike anything I've ever seen," Doctor Bittern broke in. "But I can't imagine what else it might be."

"Five folks in town have it, so far," Aaron went on, "and most of 'em are recoverin' on their own – though Mandy Smith has been walkin' a fine line, and Aubrey Malone's thin as a rail and weak as a baby." His blue eyes were clouded with worry, and Isabelle realized for the first time how deeply Aaron truly cared for his townspeople. It was this sort of love and devotion that had earned him the respect and love in return of others, like Nadine. "But little Tommy Drummond…"

"Drummond?" she said. "Is that Mitch's…"

"Brother," Aaron confirmed, nodding. "He's only six. His pa died just last year, which is why Mitch came to work for Nadine."

Her heart sank.

"His poor mother must be beside herself," she whispered. "What can I do to help?"

Once again, the two men glanced at each other.

"I told Doc Bittern how you helped me with my wound," Aaron said. "It's finally healing, after all this time. I thought maybe if you could do something for Tommy…"

Her heart sank even further, faster, and she shook her head regretfully.

"I'll do as I'm told, to help," she said, "but I have no experience with nursing, not really. Just a little bit, here and there – what Aunt Imogen taught me." She chewed on her lower lip. "If a steady pair of hands would be of any help…"

"A steady pair of hands are less useful than a steady mind," said Doctor Bittern, his voice sounding almost rusty. It was costing the man more than he wanted to let on to admit that he didn't know what to do, Isabelle realized. "We need medicine for the boy. I've done all that I can."

Isabelle turned to Aaron, her heart beginning to revive as the ideas flooded her mind. She reached out and put her hand on his; without seeming to think of it, he put his other hand over hers, closing it warmly in the middle of his own grasp, his eyes meeting hers seriously.

"Little Bear," she said.

A muscle jumped in his cheek, just enough to let her know that he knew what she meant, but he did not respond. The doctor frowned and scratched his head.

"What's that, young lady?"

She turned to him.

"The chief of the Lakota," she said. "His name is Little Bear. I've – I met him, once. His granddaughter told me that he is a healer and respected for it – that's why he's the chief, I think. He might be able to help Tommy Drummond."

Doctor Bittern was shaking his head almost before she finished speaking. Stung by this unquestioning dismissal, she frowned at him.

"Why not?" she demanded. "His knowledge of medicine may be just as great as any white man's – perhaps even greater."

Doctor Bittern waved a hand.

"It ain't that, Miss Altman," he said. "I'm man enough to admit that my knowledge has limits that might be exceeded by others, regardless of whether they live in a house or a teepee. But that's not the problem. The problem is – who among us would have the courage to go and ask?"

"I will," Isabelle said at once. "I will go. I've spoken to him once – he was peaceful to me, and friendly. I believe I could call his granddaughter something like a friend. They only want peace, too – just like the people of Millville. It's a few bad eggs who have led the attacks, and the argument could certainly be made that they had a right to defend their village."

Aaron pressed her hand.

"Isabelle..."

"I know, I know," she broke off, shaking her head. "That's not what's important now. It's Tommy – that's all. When I think of his poor mother..." She bit her lip. "If there's a chance that Little Bear may be able to help him, shouldn't we do everything we can to find out for certain? Why should we condemn that poor, innocent young boy simply because we were afraid to bridge the gap between our people and theirs?"

She waited for him to turn and look at Doctor Bittern, waited for him to tell her – gently or harshly – that she could not go back to the Lakota encampment. But instead, he took a deep breath, keeping his eyes on hers.

"All right," he said. "I reckon you're going to do it, regardless of what I or anyone else says. So I'd better go along with you."

Her eyes widened.

"Really, Aaron?"

She caught a brief flash of a grin before it disappeared.

"Well," he said, slipping her hand through his arm and turning towards the door, "only as long as you promise to protect me."

CHAPTER 8

Over and over again, as they made their way through the woods that surrounded the Indian village, Isabelle had promised both Aaron and herself that no protection would be necessary.

But now, she wasn't so sure. Instead of being met by Zonta White Bird, they were met by four sturdy young Lakota men, all of them nearly as tall as Aaron himself – and all armed. Two with hatchets, two with bows and arrows. Her eyes fled to Aaron and saw him wince, one hand covering his right arm protectively.

She stepped forward.

"Zonta?" she asked.

The young men did not look at each other, did not communicate – but some sort of signal must have passed between them that she didn't grasp, for two of them stepped aside and the other two turned. She and Aaron found themselves suddenly and unwillingly bracketed between the four, and followed along after their guides, casting glances over their shoulders at their shadows. Isabelle reached for Aaron's hand; it was a comfort to feel his fingers slide through hers, lacing together, holding her close.

"Guess they saw us comin'," he said.

This time, the village seemed deserted; as they walked through to the central building, she noted that the leather flaps that served as doors to the huts and tents were all let loose of their ties to block off the entrances. She suspected that they were tied from within; the Indians must have been warned to stay away, until their chief knew why the two townspeople had come.

She hoped that Zonta was waiting for them; as intimidated and frightened as she felt at the moment, she was not at all confident in her ability to explain their mission.

Zonta was, indeed, seated beside her grandfather in the central lodge, Isabelle noted with gratitude. She gave the younger woman a smile, but Zonta did not smile back. Her pretty face with its noble features was set in an unusual attitude of gravity; she watched without a word as Aaron and Isabelle were gestured into the low seats beside the fire. Little Bear did not look at them at all, merely peering into the fire as though it held all the answers.

Aaron's mouth opened, and Isabelle squeezed his hand hastily, willing him to keep quiet until they were spoken to. He glanced at her and closed his mouth tightly, sensing her urgency. Together, hand in hand, they sat in silence, waiting.

At last, Little Bear looked up. His eyes, Isabelle noted, were full of wariness – far more than the first time she had met him.

And – he looked tired, too.

"You are in need of something," he said. "Or you would not have come. Do you have news for me?"

Isabelle bit her lip.

"Yes – but not the news that you want, or the news that I want to give you."

He closed his eyes and sighed.

"It would be foolish to expect anything more of you," he said.

"Hey, now," Aaron burst out, frowning. "You ought to be more polite. Let the lady speak."

Little Bear regarded him – not with the animosity that Isabelle would have feared, but instead with a cold curiosity, as though a dog had suddenly learned to speak.

"Polite?" he said. At his side, his granddaughter murmured to him – an explanation in their own language, Isabelle thought – and he nodded. "Polite," he repeated. "Polite is to attack my tribe in our own home, because you white men want what does not belong to you."

Aaron sat up straight.

"It was a fight, I'll give you that," he said. "But it was your men who started it, not any of us."

"You came into our woods."

"I didn't know they were your woods. I didn't know any of it."

"You shot at us with bullets and guns."

"You shot three of us with arrows," Aaron said, jerking down the shoulder of his jacket to show the ugly scar that was forming on his upper arm. "I'm only just recovering myself. I reckon that makes us just about even."

"Even?"

"Fair and square."

"Is that how you men view such things as this?" Little Bear said heavily. "We have already lost much of our hunting grounds to Henry Parish and men like him. Three arrows found a home – is that our payment?"

Aaron flinched, but did not respond. Isabelle took a deep breath, feeling that things were going to go from bad to worse if she simply let the men do the talking.

"It isn't why we're here," she said. "I can't promise anything about Henry Parish. I'm sorry – I wish I could. But if you were willing to help us in our time of need, perhaps the people would think twice about supporting him." As quickly as she could, she explained the dire straits that Tommy Drummond was in – and the possibility of the infection spreading. "Our doctor – our healer – doesn't know what to do," she said. "We hoped that perhaps you would."

"A fever," said Little Bear, nodding. He looked to his granddaughter at his side; she watched him with bright eyes but said nothing. "Yes – I know what to do."

Isabelle sighed in relief.

"Thank you, Little Bear."

"But," he went on, "I will not do it."

Her eyes flew wide.

"What? Why not?"

"I cannot."

"But…"

"They will not agree," the old man said, turning his head

away from her. "The people of the town. They will not like it, if I come to help the boy."

"Perhaps some of them won't," she said, desperation growing in her chest. "But not all of them. The boy's mother will be very grateful, I'm sure of it."

"Suppose she does not even let me into her house?"

The fact that this was a very real possibility struck at Isabelle, but she wouldn't let it stop her now.

"You can't just believe that everyone in Millville feels the same way that Henry Parish does," she said.

"Do you speak for them?"

"I do."

"You are not from the town."

"No, I'm not – but he is."

She turned to Aaron, eyes beseeching him to speak again. He clenched his jaw, and when he spoke it was with obvious strain, though a ring of truth sounded in the words.

"What Parish and his cronies are doing is wrong," he said. "I understand now – and I reckon I could have understood before, if I'd asked the right questions. Isabelle did. She had the courage to. I guess that's something I lack. But you shouldn't hold that against all of us – just because some of us are natural cowards."

She squeezed his hand tightly in hers. His muscles felt like steel. His words seemed to go unheard by the Lakota chief.

"Why should we help?" Little Bear asked quietly. "All we ask is to be left in peace. Your people will leave us be, and we will leave you be. There is no need for help – no need for talk."

"But that's not peace at all," Isabelle cried. "It's the calm between battles, that's all it is – the silence in between gunshots." She held tightly to Aaron with one hand and reached out to Little Bear with the other. "There's been peace between you before."

Little Bear shook his head.

"Only the peace between battles, as you say," he said. "Peace is the only defense of the Indian. Anything else is to invite death."

Her heart broke a little, for she knew that he spoke the truth.

"It can be better," she said. "I know it can." She bit her lip. "Plant kindness, Little Bear, and trust that it will grow."

The old Indian watched her for a long time, hooded eyes fixed on hers. She could not read what might be going on in his mind. She could only wait.

At last, Little Bear turned to his granddaughter. He spoke a few words, and Zonta leapt to her feet, moving swiftly towards the door. Isabelle caught a flash of the girl's face and saw the familiar grin. Her heart lifted.

"I will make a remedy," Little Bear said. "It will take away the boy's fever. You will give it to him, Isabelle Altman."

She dashed tears of relief from her eyes.

"I will tell them all that you were the one who made it," she promised him. "I will tell them that you want peace with them, that you bear them no ill will."

She half expected him to contradict this – but after a moment of consideration, he simply nodded.

Zonta came back in, her arms full of pots and sticks and plants that Isabelle did not recognize. She anticipated that they would be asked to leave, and started to stand, but Little Bear gestured for her to come closer.

"Watch and see," he said.

Obediently, she crouched beside him and watched carefully as he assembled leaves and roots and water to boil on the fire, filling a large pot. As he spoke aloud, Zonta translated the names to English, murmuring them in Isabelle's ear. The girl was back to herself, now that the stressful interview between her grandfather and the white man was over. She was all smiles – and Isabelle's heart went out to her. Without quite realizing what she was doing, she flung an arm around the young Lakota girl and hugged her tightly. Zonta laughed and embraced her in return.

Her grandfather spared them only a glance before he returned to the task ahead.

When Isabelle looked at Aaron, she saw a glow of admiration in his eyes.

CHAPTER 9

Isabelle stayed up through the night. A steady pair of hands had come in handy after all, despite Doctor Bittern's dismissal of them the day before.

At first, her suggestions had been met with skepticism by everyone in the Drummond household. The matriarch of the family, Sarah Drummond, was a hollow-eyed woman of about thirty-five, thin as a rail and seeming to hold herself together by sheer force of will. It was grief that made her angry, Isabelle recognized; there was a softness in her eyes when she looked at her youngest that spoke of a mother's heart breaking into smaller pieces with each labored breath.

The townsfolk had turned out to help her in her hour of need; no fewer than a solid two dozen women of all ages crowded the little house, spilling out into the December afternoon and trading positions every half an hour, arguing over who got to watch over little Tommy now. When Isabelle arrived, she was greeted with a wary sort of warmth – wariness because she was still a relative stranger, and warmth because Aaron Granger was at her side.

Isabelle did not keep the provenance of the thick brown substance a secret – determined to do what she could to foster peaceful relations between the townsfolk and the Lakota, she told Sarah Drummond at once who had made the medicine. The news was greeted with murmurs of shock from some of the women present; Sarah Drummond eyed her fiercely.

"Am I supposed to give this to my boy, when I don't even know what's in it?"

It was unlikely that the distraught mother would have known what was in any medicine that came from a more conventional source, either, but Isabelle did not point this out. Instead, she held up the paper she had carefully written out, copying down the ingredients in the medicine as Zonta had listed them.

"Here," she said. "This is how he made it. I was there. I watched him make it – and so did Aaron."

The women murmured amongst themselves, but the tide gave no hint of turning in favor of Isabelle – or of the young boy in the little cot, tossing and muttering fitfully in his sleep. It was only when Doctor Bittern told them that it had to be worth a try that Sarah Drummond bent so far as to allow the potion to be administered.

There followed the most difficult five hours of Isabelle's life, while they all waited for the change to come.

The night passed slowly. Aaron, she supposed, must have gone home, for she did not see him among the folks that still crowded the house. Sometime before three in the morning, Sarah Drummond fell asleep at last, her worry threatening to make her sick as well; her older boy, Mitch, dozed at her side, his hand holding tightly to his mother's, as though fearful that something would snatch her away while they both slumbered.

One by one, the women drifted outside to their own homes or fell asleep in their chairs, until it was only Isabelle and a few others who kept watch over Tommy. Nadine was amongst them; Isabelle caught her watchful eyes on her more than once as the clock ticked ever closer to a frigid winter morning.

An hour before dawn, the change came.

At the sound of the cry, Sarah Drummond awoke. She came haring into Tommy's bedroom, eyes wild and hair standing up on end, to find Nadine chuckling as she patted Tommy's hand, Isabelle wiping her streaming eyes free of relieved tears, and the boy himself wide-eyed, looking among the unfamiliar faces for the beloved visage of his mother. He gave another cry at the sight of her, and she fairly leapt across the room to take him in her arms. Mitch wasn't far behind her, and Isabelle smiled through her tears to watch the overjoyed little family embrace each other.

She slipped out of the room and down the stairs, whispering the news to everyone who wakened enough to ask. Before long, the house was astir again, this time with joyful noise. Doctor Bittern was sleeping in the sitting room; he sat bolt upright as Isabelle came through and gave her a nod, as though he knew exactly what had happened.

"Well, then, Miss Altman."

She laughed a little, wiping at her eyes again, and handed over the list of ingredients to Little Bear's medicine.

"I suppose you'd better go up, Doctor Bittern, and examine the boy."

"Why should I do that, when you've been on the job?" he said dryly. "Between you and that Indian chief, I'll be out of a job before you can say Jack Robinson."

"Oh, hardly that, Doctor Bittern. Millville needs you."

"I reckon it needs you even more," he said, honesty in every word. "Courage, Aaron said – more courage than any man he's ever known. I reckon he's right about that. You've done Sarah and her family a great service, Miss Altman." He tipped his hat, which was sitting rakishly cockeyed after his impromptu napping. "But I reckon you've done the Lakota a greater one. Sarah and the rest of the women here won't forget their help in a hurry."

She bit her lip.

"And Mitch Drummond?" she said. "He's one of the biggest supporters of Henry Parish, from what I can tell. Do you suppose this might change his mind?"

The doctor eyed her seriously for a moment.

"Now, Miss Altman," he said, "let's not shoot the moon."

She nodded and went out the front door. Though it was still frosty outside, the skies were dark and clear, stars shining brightly. The moon that she had been warned not to shoot was down; dawn was only a few hours away. She took a deep breath and breathed a silent prayer to the heavens – a prayer of thanks, and a request for a further blessing even than she had already been given.

Something stirred in the darkness, and she leapt, a hand going to her throat – then laughed as she recognized what it was.

Who it was.

"I thought you went home."

"I did." Aaron came up the stairs of the veranda and stood beside her, hands in his pockets, watching the skies. "Just long enough to see to the cattle. Then I came back. Tommy's all right, isn't he?"

She took a deep breath and nodded.

"Yes, praise be. He'll be just fine."

"That potion did it. Little Bear's medicine."

"Yes, I believe it did."

"Wouldn't have happened without you. He might have died."

She shivered and drew her cloak closer around her. He stepped towards her and put an arm around her, as casual and unassuming as though they had known each other for decades instead of just a few weeks. As though they were married already.

"I don't like to think of it – Aaron, what can we do about Henry Parish?"

He turned his head to look down at her, eyebrows raised in astonishment.

"Why, just like you told Little Bear – we can't promise anything. It's up to him what he does."

"But the town supports him."

"That's up to the town, too."

"But the change has to start somewhere," she argued. "I know that there's fighting between Indians and settlers all across America, but surely…"

"It's been worse other places," Aaron said, running a hand through his sandy hair. "Far worse than here. Millville has its problems, that's for sure, but they're – they're small. Compared to some."

Isabelle shook her head.

"No," she said.

"No?" Aaron repeated, raising an eyebrow.

"A small problem is gossip in a big town," she said. "A small problem is feeling that the opinion of others should shape your life, change it for better or for worse – even if it's based on nothing more than rumor. This, Aaron – this is a matter of peace, of unity. It's important. There's nothing small about it."

He smiled at her, a little ruefully.

"I know," he said. "All I meant is that the fighting between us and the Lakota – well, no one's been killed. Other places aren't so lucky."

"And when Millville was first founded?" she pressed. "Fifty years ago, when the settlers first found this little valley and took half of it from Little Bear and his people? Was no one killed then?"

Aaron's smile disappeared as he sobered.

"I guess I don't know that for sure," he said. "They don't write about towns like Millville in the history books."

She shook her head. "No – but it is part of history, all the same."

He rubbed his chin. "History – and history repeats itself, they say. So, we might achieve a little peace with Little Bear and the rest, carve out a little time of quiet. Who's to say that the fights won't happen again? Henry Parish is only one man, but there are plenty more like him. Even if he decided to leave well enough alone, there's nothing stopping others from following in his footsteps."

"Perhaps," she allowed. "But that doesn't mean it isn't worth a try, all the same." She looked at him, her heart racing as it always did when they stood near each other. Aaron Granger – the handsome rancher she'd been matched with by a matrimonial agency, the man she was going to marry, and most importantly, the man she loved. Even if he did have a lot to learn. "Do you know what my Aunt Imogen always said?" she asked quietly. "She said that striking out for the new would always replace the old – if we would only let it."

She gestured to the town, her hand closing into a fist and then opening as though to scatter seed, a movement she had seen from Zonta – and she could imagine all too easily Little Bear making the same gesture. *Plant kindness, and watch it grow, Aaron.* "It doesn't have to be like this – just because it always has been, up until now. We can have a new way, tomorrow. We could start right now."

They stood in silence for a long moment, letting the possibility stretch out before them.

"Aunt Imogen was the one who suggested I apply to the matrimonial agency," Isabelle said at last.

Aaron's eyes found hers, his arm warm around her.

"Good old Aunt Imogen," he whispered.

There in the dark, with nothing but the stars to witness, he leaned down to kiss her for the first time – and there would be more, Isabelle knew, with a little thrill of certainty running through her.

As soon as all this was settled.

CHAPTER 10

Doctor Bittern stared at Isabelle, his pipe forgotten in his hand.

"You're going to do what?"

"Throw a party," Isabelle said with determination. "To celebrate the new year."

"But that's only two days away."

"I know it."

"What sort of party?"

"A big one. Everyone will be there. All the town. And…" She took a deep breath. "I'm going to invite the Lakota."

Doctor Bittern looked from Isabelle to Aaron, who sat beside her on the sofa in Sarah Drummond's tiny sitting room.

Though Tommy was well on the way to recovery, half the town still had the habit of drifting through the Drummond household to check in on him, even a week after the fever had broken. Isabelle had looked for Doctor Bittern at his own home and office first, then had gone straight there, knowing that if he wasn't there already then, he likely would arrive before too long.

In response to the doctor's inquiring glance, Aaron merely shrugged.

"I know it's early days yet," the doctor said, "but forgive me if I point out that you've evidently already learned not to question Miss Altman when she makes a decision."

"Oh, I knew that from the first day I met her," Aaron said fervently.

Isabelle nudged him with her elbow, but she was smiling.

"Smart man," said Doctor Bittern, approvingly. "But I'm sorry to tell you, Isabelle, I'm not sure how folks will respond to you steppin' in and makin' decisions for all of us."

Isabelle lifted her chin.

"Why not?" she said. "Everyone was glad enough to let Henry Parish make decisions for the whole town. He's told you all what you're entitled to, and no one has yet told him no. He's not a local any more than I am. And what's more – he's wrong, and I'm right."

The doctor shook his head, but he was smiling, too.

"I know it, I know it," he said. "I don't have any quibble with your reasoning, Miss Altman. Just pointin' out the facts. Besides – how on earth are you going to organize a big party like that in just a few days?"

"We'll all help," said a voice from the doorway. Sarah Drummond stepped into the room. Her eyes were no less full of fire, her frame still almost sickly in its thinness, but her face had regained both love and softness, now that her youngest son was safe. "It won't be easy, I reckon, but we'll do our part. Those of us that understand." Her eyes fixed on Isabelle, and she nodded. There was respect in that acknowledgement, and Isabelle felt a little shiver go down her spine.

For the three weeks she had lived in Millville, she had done her best to make herself a part of the town. Now, at last, she had succeeded – and it was not only in spite of her communication with the Lakota, but it was also because of it. Doctor Bittern was right; the people of Millville would not be quick to forget.

Behind Sarah, the figure of Mitch Drummond slipped swiftly by, silently, and went out the front door.

The doctor and Aaron faded into the background as Isabelle joined forces anew with Sarah Drummond. As they made their plans, other women trickled into the house, drawn by the need to see how Tommy was doing, and caught one by one by Sarah, who towed them into the sitting room until it was stuffed as full as it been the night that Tommy's fever had broken. In no uncertain terms, Sarah told each one what her role in the production would be, delegating food and decorations left and right. And to each one, she explained that the gathering would be not just for the people of Millville, but for their nearest neighbors, the Lakota.

By the time Isabelle and Aaron escaped into the gathering twilight, she was half giddy with relief and exhaustion, and it was three hours later.

"Can you imagine?" she asked Aaron, slipping her arm through his. "Why, I do believe that Sarah Drummond could have organized the whole thing single-handedly. And I half expect that she will go to every house in all of Millville and personally escort them to the party." She laughed. "The looks on some of their faces when she said the Lakota were coming…"

Aaron shook his head, grinning.

"It was a shock, that's for sure."

"I wish I had the courage that Sarah Drummond has."

He stopped and turned to her, taking both her hands in his.

"Isabelle Altman," he said, "you have more courage than anyone I've ever met."

He leaned down, and she let her eyes drift closed; her toes tingled in anticipation of his kiss. But there was a shout from down the street, a voice that seemed vaguely familiar, and she opened her eyes and turned to look.

Her heart sank. She knew that face – though she had only seen him once before.

Aaron's mouth tightened into a thin line.

"Henry Parish," he said.

Parish advanced on them, waving his hat with a jovial grin. He was a good decade, possibly even two, older than Aaron, and had some fifty pounds on the younger man. There was a weakness to his chin that Isabelle disliked – but perhaps, she had to admit, such a judgement was unfair on her part. After all, she already knew she disliked him. His looks really had nothing to do with it.

Aaron folded his arms.

"Out and about without your posse, Parish?"

"Why, you're my posse, Aaron," said the older man genially. He gave Isabelle a curt nod, barely even polite, and returned his attention to the man at her side. "I just heard from young Mitch Drummond that you and the young lady here took an excursion straight into the heart of the enemy camp."

"I beg your pardon?" Isabelle said frostily.

He ignored her.

"Matter of fact, sounds like you managed to make a connection with the old man himself."

"I didn't do a thing," Aaron said. "Isabelle's the one who started to build the bridge."

"Well, well. Isabelle, eh?" For the first time, Isabelle felt Henry Parish's eyes settle on hers. They were shiny and black, like the back of a beetle. She didn't care for the sensation and tucked her arm more firmly into Aaron's. "Then we have you to thank for our window of opportunity."

"What are you talkin' about, Parish?"

"Why, I'm talkin' action, Aaron. If we strike now, they'll never see it coming. Just imagine it – that old chief of theirs will be congratulating himself over makin' inroads with the local population, thinkin' that it'll all be smooth sailing from here on out. They'll be restin' on their laurels." He pressed a hand on Aaron's free arm, leaning into him, eyes gleaming. "Thinkin' they've bought themselves some leeway with that medicine that cured the kid – thinkin' that we owe 'em one, now. They'll never expect it when we go to attack. This is the time to take the village and chase those Indians out of our territory once and for all."

Isabelle caught a glimpse of Aaron's face and covered her mouth with her hand. She had never seen such rage on his handsome face – rage and disdain. He looked at Henry Parish as though the wealthy rancher was something he'd scraped off his shoe, which had then suggested that Aaron join a crusade on his behalf.

"You listen here, Henry Parish," he said, his voice full of cold fury. "I made a mistake in supporting you the first time, thinkin' that you were within your rights to lay claim to land. Well, that land belonged to someone well before you ever laid eyes on it, and I'll be damned if I'll stand by your side again while you try to take somethin' that doesn't belong to you.

Every man's got to do what he feels is right, and if others in town take your side, then I guess I don't have anything to say about it. But you just remember, Parish – every man has to make his peace with God, when his day comes." His lip curled. "And I don't reckon that God will be wanting much peace with you."

His hand slipped down to find Isabelle's, holding it firmly, and he turned away, towing her after him. She spared one glance over her shoulder at the wealthy rancher, who was staring after them. His façade of geniality and eagerness had drained away, leaving anger – and a flat whiteness that looked almost like fear.

Aaron was one of the most well-respected men in Millville. If he snubbed Henry Parish and refused to support his schemes, there would be others who were quick to follow.

She held tightly to his hand as he kept pressing forward. It wasn't until they were several blocks away and had turned the corner that he suddenly stopped, bringing her up beside him.

"Let's get married," he said.

She gaped up at him.

"Wh – what?"

"You did plan on marryin' me when you came here, right?"

"Yes, but – but you said we had to wait until it was all settled, and…"

"It is settled," Aaron said firmly. "Danger or not, it's settled as far as I'm concerned. I need your courage, Isabelle Altman – will you share it with me?" He laced his fingers through hers, gently. "Will you share your life with me?"

Isabelle's eyes filled with tears.

"What's left to share?" she breathed. "Everything I have is already yours."

There in the street, Aaron leaned down to kiss her, arms around her firmly. It was the early evening, and the town was rife with passers-by, all of them full of curiosity and opinions.

Aaron didn't seem to mind.

And to Isabelle's amusement, she didn't mind, either.

. . .

It took all of Sarah's energies to bring the new year's party to life – but in the end, two days later, everything was just as Isabelle had planned.

It had snowed the day before; but today, New Year's Day, the early afternoon skies were a brilliant blue, the sun dazzling off the pristine snow. The little town of Millville had never looked so picturesque – even though it was empty.

Town was empty, and all the townsfolk were there in the little town hall.

Those who had been charged with the decorating of the town hall had outdone themselves, especially considering how little time they had to bring it all together. Isabelle suspected that there were more than a few decorations borrowed from earlier Christmas parties – but it didn't matter. There were wreathes and winter flowers and greenery everywhere she looked; three dozen candles and oil lamps glittered on every surface, working with the roaring fire in the fireplace to keep the hall warm despite the open doors. She'd wanted the doors to remain open as long as possible, barring any bad weather – to make sure that the inside of the hall looked inviting to all who passed by it.

That was the one thing that was not as perfect as she had hoped – not a single Lakota had come.

She'd delivered the invitation in person, with Zonta at her side. Little Bear had taken it with little more than a nod of acknowledgement; even his brief murmur of thanks had spoken volumes about his reluctance. Still, she had hoped that, in the end, he might follow up on the peace she had asked him to make – the real peace. A step forward, as it were, on the bridge that she had worked so hard to build.

But she had to admit, the townsfolk were likely more at ease celebrating by themselves without the Lakota.

Still, it saddened her heart that her good intentions had been so thoroughly contravened – until she happened to spot a familiar figure stepping through the open doorway.

"Zonta."

Isabelle rushed forward to the girl, clasping her hands in her own, beaming at her. She felt as though she were greeting an old friend – as though it were Aunt Imogen herself who was here. If only the people of the town could feel that same way about the Lakota.

And if only the Lakota could feel the same way about the townsfolk…

"It is beautiful," Zonta said, gazing around herself with admiration. "I did not think."

"Everyone worked very hard on it," Isabelle said. "And now we're enjoying the fruits of our labors. It's the new year – a new beginning."

Zonta shook her head, smiling.

"For us, it is not the new year," she said.

"Oh," said Isabelle, feeling rather deflated. Zonta squeezed her hand encouragingly.

"But a new beginning, yes," she said. "Always a new beginning."

Isabelle mustered up her own spirits and nodded, managing another smile. "I'm glad to see you. Are you alone?"

"Yes, I am alone."

"Did you –" Worry grabbed at her heart. "You didn't have to sneak away from home, did

you? I mean – your grandfather didn't forbid you to come to town?"

Zonta laughed.

"Of course not," she said. "I told him I wanted to come to your celebration, to see my friend Isabelle. He said, 'Yes, but be home before the wolves howl.'"

"I…see…and…when is that?"

"Nine o'clock," said Zonta seriously.

Isabelle bit her lip to keep from smiling, until she realized that Zonta was teasing her. They chuckled together.

"I'd hoped that your grandfather would come," she admitted. "That – well – that your whole village would come. I intended this celebration for them as well as for us." She paused; *them and us* was wrong. "For all of us," she corrected herself.

Zonta White Bird gave her one of her wide, familiar smiles.

"This is the first day," she said. "The first time. Little Bear gave me permission to come here. For the first day, perhaps, that is enough."

Isabelle thought this over, nodding, and then gave her a smile in return.

"Yes," she said. "Do not despise the day of small beginnings, as the good book says – let's not shoot the moon."

Zonta tilted her head curiously, and Isabelle laughed.

"It just means to take things one step at a time and be grateful for what we have rather than asking for everything at once."

Zonta nodded, and as they went on deeper into the crowd, Isabelle caught her murmuring the words to herself thoughtfully. *"Shoot the moon...shoot the moon..."*

Isabelle smiled and put an arm around the girl, hugging her fondly.

"Aaron and I will be married soon," she said. "Perhaps your grandfather will attend our wedding."

Zonta gave her another gleaming smile.

"Perhaps," she agreed, with a nod. And then she was off into the crowd of townsfolk, tilting her head curiously this way and that at each piece of newness that she encountered. The last Isabelle saw of her was that she had linked arms with a few of the young girls from town and joined them in their dance.

Aaron was at her side before she saw him coming. He smiled down at her.

"I heard that," he said. "Invitin' the Lakota to our wedding, are you? And here we haven't even set a date for it."

She smiled back up at him, refusing to feel embarrassed.

"I know it," she said. "But I have a feeling that we will, before long. After all – the trouble may not be settled, but we are. Aren't we, Aaron Granger?"

He swept her into his arms, leaning down to whisper in her ear.

"I don't know about you, Miss Altman, but I'm not settlin' – I plan to shoot the moon."

As she lost herself in his kiss once more, Isabelle couldn't help but think of the future and what it might hold for her, here in Millville. There was peace to be made, families to be started, unions to be joined. There were seeds of kindness to be planted – by herself and Aaron both, hand in hand.

"But we *can* invite Little Bear and the Lakota to our wedding, can't we?" she asked, when her mouth was free once more.

Aaron laughed.

"Why not," he said. "The more, the merrier."

As they moved together out into the dance, Isabelle wondered whether Little Bear might really come to their wedding. There was a good chance that she wouldn't see him, even if he did – perhaps he would be just behind the tree line, watching, nodding to himself with that small smile of approval.

It would be just the beginning.

And that, she knew, was enough.

The End

CONTINUE READING...

Thank you for reading *The Bride Takes a Stand!* Are you wondering **what to read next?** Why not read *The Livery Bride?* Here's a peek for you:

1892 Boston, Massachusetts

"Miss Holt." The tall grey-haired man hunched under a heavy overcoat looked at her with sad weary eyes as Jennifer stood holding the front door of the house open.

"Mister Harley," she greeted him with as much enthusiasm as his own. "Please, come in."

"Much as I despise being the bearer of bad news once more, my dear, I regret to inform you that the one week you were allowed to find other lodgings and vacate this house ends today at noon." Edward Harley, the family lawyer for the

Holts, looked apologetic. "You must leave this house and the surrounding property immediately. The men will be over here by noon today to stake their claims on it."

"But, but, Mister Harley..." Jennifer all but wept. "Where will I go? This is my home. Papa was all the family I had. I have nowhere else in the world to go."

"Your father was a good friend of mine, my dear." Harley reached over and took her trembling hands in his. "His sudden passing comes as a shock to me as much as it does to you, but my hands are tied. It is the law of the land. Milton owed many debts to many people, and he hasn't made even the minimum payments in the last four months. The courts have ruled that in lieu of the outstanding debts, this house and all relevant property and holdings of your late father now belong to the men he owed."

"I couldn't find anywhere else to go." Jennifer sat down on the couch next to the door. "I don't know anyone who can..."

"Do you have any family or perhaps friends who could take you in?" the lawyer asked her in earnest.

"I have no family that I know of." She shook her head. "And as for friends, I would guess they were only my friends when I was on equal status with them. Now that I am penniless and am going to be homeless, I'm sure none of them want to even see me."

"Such a sad world we live in." Edward Harley shook his balding head.

"I don't know what to do, Mister Harley." Jennifer covered her face with her palms. "I have no money, I have no one…"

"You might find someone," Harley offered in suggestion. "A man, I mean, whom you can marry and find some stability."

Visit HERE To Read More!

https://ticahousepublishing.com/mail-order-brides.html

THANKS FOR READING!

If you **love Mail Order Bride Romance**, **Visit Here**

https://wesrom.subscribemenow.com/

to find out about all **New Susannah Calloway Romance Releases! We will let you know as soon as they become available!**

If you enjoyed *The Bride Takes a Stand*, would you kindly take a couple minutes to leave a positive review on Amazon? It only takes a moment, and positive reviews truly make a difference. Thank you so much! I appreciate it!

Turn the page to discover more Mail Order Bride Romances just for you!

MORE MAIL ORDER BRIDE
ROMANCES FOR YOU!

We love clean, sweet, adventurous Mail Order Bride Romances and have a lovely library of Susannah Calloway titles just for you!

Box Sets — A Wonderful Bargain for You!

https://ticahousepublishing.com/bargains-mob-box-sets.html

Or enjoy Susannah's single titles. You're sure to find many favorites! (Remember all of them can be downloaded FREE with Kindle Unlimited!)

Sweet Mail Order Bride Romances!

https://ticahousepublishing.com/mail-order-brides.html

ABOUT THE AUTHOR

Susannah has always been intrigued with the Western movement - prairie days, mail-order brides, the gold rush, frontier life! As a writer, she's excited to combine her love of story with her love of all that is Western. Presently, Susannah lives in Wyoming with her hubby and their three amazing children.

www.ticahousepublishing.com
contact@ticahousepublishing.com